THE RIVER BENDS IN TIME

GLEN A. MAZIS

ANAPHORA LITERARY PRESS

COCHRAN, GEORGIA

Anaphora Literary Press
163 Lucas Rd., Apt. I-2
Cochran, GA 31014
www.anaphoraliterary.wordpress.com

Book design by Anna Faktorovich, Ph.D.

Copyrights © 2012 by Glen A. Mazis

All rights reserved. No part of this book may be reproduced in any form or by any electronic or mechanical means, including information storage and retrieval systems, without permission in writing from Glen A. Mazis. Writers are welcome to quote brief passages in their critical studies, as American copyrights law dictates.

Cover Image: "Fortnum & Mason" by Camille Pissarro (Fox Hill, Upper Norwood), photo by Harry Lawford.

Proofread by: Emily E. Crawford-Margison

Published in 2012 by Anaphora Literary Press

The River Bends in Time
Glen A. Mazis—1st edition.

ISBN-13: 978-1-937536-23-7
ISBN-10: 1-937536-23-8

Library of Congress Control Number: 2012933922

THE RIVER BENDS IN TIME

———————————

GLEN A. MAZIS

OTHER BOOKS BY MAZIS:

Emotion and Embodiment (Peter Lang, 1993)

Trickster, Magician, & Grieving Man (Inner Traditions, 1994)

Earthbodies: Rediscovering our Planetary Senses (SUNY Press, July, 2002)

Humans/Animals/Machines: Blurred Boundaries (SUNY Press, Fall, 2008)

The Depth of the Sensual Face of the World (In Development…)

Contents

Acknowledgments — 9

I. Quiet Moments along the Susquehanna — 11

Two Winter Deaths — 13
Rivers of Time and Snow — 14
The Gustatory Zeal of Falling Snow — 15
On this Path of Transubstantiation — 16
Restored Silk Mill Apartment — 17
Stepping into Different Waters — 18
Neighbor Gone — 20
Small Town Estate Auction — 22
Talking and Nodding Silences — 24
Back Fence Salvation — 26
The Halloween Helicopter Misses the Canal House — 28
Pennsylvania Church House Farewell — 29
Moving to California — 31
Moving Back after Two years in California — 32
Ducks like Slanted Rain from the Sky — 33
Running Under the Snow Geese — 34
Living by the Railroad Tracks — 35
Susquehanna Floods and the Fullness of Breasts — 36
October Monsoon — 37
A Pond behind the Susquehanna Canal House — 38
Wood Pile Love Song — 41

II. The Past is Lost — 43

The Extinction of the Tall Tale — 45
Arroyo Seco Canyon Restaurant Dog — 47
Alzheimer's Railway Conductor — 49
How the Word Lost its Voice — 50
The Famous Artificial Heart Experiment — 51
Cyberspace Theology — 53
Deprivation Tournament — 54
Babi Yar — 56

A Generation of Boys Who Love Terror	57
September Eleventh of a New Millennium	58
The Appalachian Space of this Eternal Return	59
The Gravity that Pulls Us through the Floor	61
The Lost Fossil Fuel of Passion	63
Morning Memories	65

III. To the Edge of Return   67

When the Doctor Said Cancer	69
A Week after Colon Cancer Stage IV Discovered	70
Nothing to Say	72
Caught Suddenly Dying in a Dream	73
Six Days of Sailing towards the Moon	75
Sailing towards the Light	77
The Asymptote of Loss	79
Full Body Pet Scan	80
Preoperative Sutra	82
To the Edge and Back	84

IV. Futures to Reawaken the Past   87

The Last Train to the Heart	89
The Body of the Dark	90
Poor Boys, Rare Tortoises, and Existential Choices	92
Van Gogh at Arles	94
Van Gogh at St. Remy	95
Monet's Water Lilies of Paris	96
The Loneliness of Book Writing	97
The Ancient Root	99
Pelicans of South Laguna Beach	101
The Alchemical Secret of Movement	102
San Juan Capistrano Mission	104
The Natural Power of Memory	106
The Other Time of Encounter	107

ACKNOWLEDGMENTS

Grateful acknowledgment is made to the editors of *Object 1:4* (Lancaster, PA: Zero Degree Press, 1977), a chapbook of PA poets, for the first publication of "Van Gogh at St. Remy"; of *Afterthoughts* for "The Generation of Boys Who Love Terror;" of *Asheville Poetry Review: (BEST OF 1994-2004)* for "Six Days Sailing towards the Moon," "The Alchemical Secret of Movement," of *Atlanta Review* for "Moving to California;" of *California Quarterly* for "Morning Memories;" of the *Cedar Hill Review* for "Babi Yar;" of the *Central PA Magazine* for "September Eleventh of the New Millennium" (also for the *Philadelphia Inquirer* for the same poem); of *The Comstock Review* for "The Extinction of the Tall Tale;" of *Concho River Review* for "Small Town Estate Auction" and "Alzheimer's Railway Conductor;" of *Connecticut River Review* for "The Ancient Root;" of *Cumberland Poetry Review* for "Cyberspace Theology," of *Ellipsis* for "Inexorably Marching Time and the other Time of Encounter," "Two Winter Deaths," "Living by the Railroad Tracks," "Ducks like Slanted Rain from the Sky"; of *Great Midwestern Quarterly* for "The Appalachian Space of this Eternal Return"; of *The Poet's Guild* for "Van Gogh at Arles," "Van Gogh at St. Remy"; of *Mangrove* for "The Lost Fossil Fuel of Passion"; of *Many Mountains Moving* for "The Famous Artificial Heart Experiment"; of *North American Review* for "Preoperative Sutra"; of *River Oak Review* "Neighbor Gone," "A Week after Colon Cancer Stage IV Discovered," "Back Fence Salvation" "Pennsylvania Church House Farewell," and "An Auto Mechanic Escapes Appalachia"; of *Riverrun* for "How the Word Lost its Voice"; of *Rosebud* for "Rivers of Time and Snow"; of the *South Dakota Review* for "San Juan Capistrano Mission," "Bank Swallows and Strainers," and "Pelicans at South Laguna Beach," of *The Spoon River Poetry Review* for "This Path of Transubstantiation," and "Restored Silk Mill Apartment," of *Sou'Wester* for "Nothing to Say," of *Worcester Review* for "Monet's Water Lilies of Paris"; of *Writer's Forum* for "Arroyo Seco Canyon Restaurant Dog" "Full Body Pet Scan," and "The Loneliness of Book Writing," of *Willow Review* for "The Gravity that Pulls Us through the Floor," of *Wisconsin Review* for "Suddenly Dying Caught in Dream," of *Xanadu* for "Deprivation Tournament"; also "Inexorably Marching Time and the other Time of Encounter" was republished in *Earthbodies* (SUNY Press: Albany, 2002).

I. Quiet Moments along the Susquehanna

Two Winter Deaths

I heard the mouse settle into a porcelain cup
and felt the hurt and the tired
resignation of resting
when all hope dies
the misguided search for thistle seeds
kept sealed within the plastic below
had spent the last of his garnered
winter soul a trek beyond himself
that would cost this turn
on the wheel of rebirth.

Kali in a cupboard
ignored as an imagined lapse
of attention to reading or was it
looking deeply into your eyes
when I thought you'd take
all the seeds of my long stored
winter's kernels of love and hope
and make your home in my house
if I kept giving you the seeds
—I knew the field creature
would have loved to stay.

So steady in my love
I listened for each of your sighs
to get more tins about for you
before you'd know you were hungry,
and missed your scratching, scratching.
Only when you left suddenly,
I thought to take some tea
from a special china cup
I lifted to my lips
his small body curled
within a hope of welcome.

Rivers of Time and Snow

In the midst of the Nor'easter, snowflakes swirl
slowly as if each is suspended from a parachute,
flakes like frail white arms reaching up to hold on
as spinning on silken threads they descend quietly,
pure centers of time released from heavens above.

Within the woods, moments cease running away
in a receding parade out of reach. All around us,
the instants fall heavy and soft like lovers into bed.
So many spill into our hearts, we feel full like
the woods tonight;
patient in the swell of perfect silence.

The Gustatory Zeal of Falling Snow

As the towhee's cry is slurped up into stillness
by the white tongue of snow spreading serpentine
over cars and hills as it fattens itself,
applies to surfaces, tastes oil slicks and marsh grass,
scotch pines and smoke from chimneys rise.

Where streaming rickety waters creak over
slumbering salamanders, they carve
a laceration in the white fervent skin,
but deftly done, to prevent snow from devouring
the river and so halting the cannibal temptations
within the watery tribe.

A wooden church has never been so savory
to lost souls as it is to this tongue
that never wags in penitence,
nor has the old woman slipping in fear
at being insistently licked
felt for decades on her wrinkled skin
a caress driven to cover her completely
and melt with her.

The leftovers in the dumpster, the homeless
on the streets, the chemicals oozing from drains,
the mash of debris underfoot,
and the tears of the abandoned we are loathe to take
into our mouths and taste their plight
are swallowed completely without hesitation
by this seemingly cold winter,
who finds them all to be its sacrament.

On this Path of Transubstantiation

Lope, lope, I move through the skies
with each runner's footfall
unable to translate
for my sedentary friends
how earth becomes sky,
but flying isn't about altitude

the moment when warm muscles
melt the frost accumulated over night
on the mind's windshield,
so kids skipping down the street,
dogs looking for the right place to pee,
the truck lumbering through the gears
like a rhinoceros lifting out of the mud

can be seen for themselves
gathering into themselves
intricate, irreplaceable dance steps
in an incantatory daily ritual
that makes the divinities of the sky
the pedestrians of the earth,
then having turned it all up and back
these steps have broken
the earth's gravity.

Restored Silk Mill Apartment

As I try to sleep, the glowing angels
are glued to the fifteen foot
ceilings. The factory windows peer

out at the unraveling river.
A border of phosphorescence
rings the dark walls

as the century-old silk worms
shine with continued effort
to spin the slinky thread.

Only now, there are no gathered looms,
no floors packed with women
married to the insect.

A heavenly choir
who gave their substance
for our wardrobes

sings to me at midnight
how others can make their home
in the spinning of your body.

Stepping into Different Waters

Heraclitus never said that one cannot step
into the same river twice,
rather he said we always step
into ever different waters
yet the river remains, he claimed,
perhaps at the edge of this town.

For a man who asked that his corpse
be thrown onto the garbage pile,
this saying was a timid yes to the public
who thought him crazy no matter,
for we know there is no river to return to
other than waters always slipping away.

It is not going to new places that make always
new waters, but how they become
what they were not in some new time
like falling from the sky to farmers' delight
or becoming whispering steam from the tea kettle
or syrupy sap from maples to tap in the fall.

Twenty years in this town watching lives slip
into the waters of no more,
seeing the young skipping girl who now limps,
the stores that are shuttered,
the restaurants that only serve
the field mice dining at empty tables,
yet also the pile of slats on a foundation,
the neighborhood tavern of unquiet ghosts,
rebuilt into the town's happening place,
cars parked all along the river,
I wonder at the way back home.

I think I'll have to find another
path if I want to return, not retracing
the old one, since it slopes away into the river
whose bed has changed several times like mine
with seasonal floods of mud and old furniture.
Yet, around the S-bend encircling the town
often comes the same flock of great blue herons
who have perfected their flapping,
slow, dancing walk onto the waters—
turning the river's flow
into one long dance floor.

Neighbor Gone

George spent half a century inspecting
the concrete ribs and electrical veins
of buildings, learning how the odd coincidence
of things placed together can poison
the workings behind the edifice.
Buildings also have seasons of
despair and breakdown,
hold onto a distant past
until clouds of poison gather
behind walls and fumes burst into flame.

George's keen sense of proximity seemed
to make him cherish his neighbors
as if each were a link in an electrical
line going down the street,
our homes like layered insulation,
each house piled against each other
like fibers packed in against the cold.
A family shouting three houses down
was like a short in the wiring
to make us buzz and snap
and the light among us would flicker and stop.

He'd splice the couple's differences
and keep all of us connected,
even the solitary ones like me.
The dinners he left on my doorstep
when I came home late from work
made me feel like I lived
in an Irish forest with helpful
lurking leprechauns.

George saw me through visions
of the good deeds and folk
of the Old Testament, of people
reading books he'd longed to read.
He called me his professor
and said it was an honor to talk.
I couldn't always fill the role
of wandering spirit thirsting
for knowledge, undaunted
by the hordes closing in on the Israelites,
but he never noticed I carried
more books than I read.

His respect glowed like little lanterns
placed carefully between our houses.
In each casserole dish left
at night steamed friendship,
so my steps home through these dingy
backwater town streets
became a rustling through leaves
in an enchanted wood.
When George was gone,
all our places in this small town
seemed to move further apart.

Small Town Estate Auction

Frank's house lost its paint every two years,
stripped by the same factory fumes
that would burn away the linings of his lungs.
At least the factory, a block away,
kept wheezing its acrid breath,
whereas the remains of the town's textile mill
stands in a new growth forest, its bricks
overgrown with honeysuckle and daisies,
a favorite spot for hikers on the river path.

Now that Frank has worked his last shift,
neighbors gather in patched jeans,
overalls, with a thermos of coffee,
most out to enjoy a sunny morning, but
some on the way home from night shifts
to the only memorial most will have,
since even the church has closed down
and the downtown restaurant was shut
by the IRS, who auctioned off the owner's
goldfish from the tank in the dining room,
along with a half dozen tomatoes
still sitting on the cutting board.

Antiqued green shelves, fiberboard,
fake wooden furniture, rusty tools,
ragged chairs, sagging trestle tables,
tarnished steel forks,
trail through the middle of the
leaning house like a row of weary
workers waiting to get out the back
kitchen door to the table top
where the auctioneer finally
furloughs them from their contract
with a man drinking his coffee at five
a.m. or p.m. in the same foggy light,
brought home with him from the factory
that seeps out of his bulging hems.

The hems didn't always bulge
when the belly was sleeker with more
to eat, to boast of, to feel proud of,
but grew when suppers got lean,
when Mildred wouldn't sew another hem
to contain the beer barrel stomach
that belched violence for her
and vapors of hate for him;
hate for those shuttered storefronts,
hate for those shiny accountant boys
running the shop,
hate for the hours
sitting at this table
auctioning off his life in his mind
to these sonafabitches.

Now in the Spring sunlight, the things
that surrounded those last years
find new homes sitting on this table
accompanied by an auctioneer's song.
Looking sideways, buying cheap
these last bits and pieces,
the neighbors know
they should be piled on Main Street
for some memorial of possessions
never owned.

Talking and Nodding Silences

South Central Pennsylvania is puzzling
how it lies further south
than the Deep South.
Bowed men's faces focus on trouser cuffs,
blond girls bursting tight tops walk strollers
with lips pressed, boys gather in front
of broken windowed storefronts,
but turn their backs to the road,
as a knock on the door resounds through Main Street,
since families are busy out back
hiding what might be found out by strangers.

In the talkative true South, sterling drawls
burble on each street corner.
Stories within stories flow
more faithfully than the Mississippi.
Like the logs in mid-current,
some things pass by unnoticed.
Rules of how to be and with whom mix
among pretty words but at a higher pitch,
like the dog's hypersonic whistle,
so outsiders can't hear.
It is considerable art
to keep things hidden in the midst
of what you display
for all to delight in.

But deep in the Pennsylvania soil of steel and coal,
a forsaken tuber rots like a sore
beneath the skin
that needs the light of day.
Wound into its kernel are night visits
by miners to their daughters,
women leaping into the shaft after husbands
who didn't return, and their boys
taking pickaxes as the alphabet.
The soil here is rich and black,
but who would want to tell you
how it got that way?

Back Fence Salvation

Somehow, it seemed perfectly backwater:
the old diner sign broken off its pedestal
and dragged around back for safekeeping.
Now, customers drugged by the sleepy
town can drive by unmolested
without their eyes blinking
food, diner, food, diner,
suddenly hearing the groans
of their tired stomachs,
exhausted among factory landscapes
rusting with pipes, benches, vises—
peptic despair over finding an oasis
among abandoned assembly lines, water
towers, and congregations assembled.

The last theft, four years ago,
Twenty-three dollars of magazines
from the stand, unguarded.
Were they sold in the back of bars,
hot legs and homemaker recipes?
Probably venture capital for seed
or stuffing for an open wall
or the library of lazy decades.
If I talked to the manager, he'd be mad:
"What's wrong with customers
that won't look around the back,
nothing can be seen out front.
Don't people know psychology
or at least their neighbors?"

Then, he'd look off to the sky and add:
"You put it behind, lean it on the fence
and it goes, flies north with the geese,
lands on the river later, but with so
many others squawking, nobody hears.
Then it's safe for it to land back in
the fields again, geese as far as the eye
sees: spitting out the seeds which get buried.
In the spring, our faith gets rewarded
when the geese fly overhead. All these
rusty parts around here grow new skins
and become shiny chrome mirrors to God,
reflecting the goodness of what was forgot
and the way to the diner for Easter dinner."

The Halloween Helicopter Misses the Canal House

As the little ghouls and aliens and mobsters scurry from
Halloween house to house, the put, put, put, slows and
clanks as the huge metal dragonfly sails over my two
hundred year old house and into the Susquehanna.
Seemingly most frantic for a treat, it gave us a trick.

No doubt the student pilot had turned to the flight teacher
to ask for a Hershey's while she reached into her bag, as the
current loomed closer and closer, and dragged them under.
In small river towns on these dark nights, we expect the goblins
like hypnotized catfish from the river's bottom to sail over

our roofs, mouths agape and empty eyes blazing, or to see
the shimmering white dress of the ghost left at the altar
centuries ago, having traveled by rail to her appointed
union with the canal man who drifted downstream right past.
But we're not ready for metal ships to fall from the sky
unless it's an old canal boat that got lost in the
clouds and is coming home to put into dock.

Pennsylvania Church House Farewell

The plank floors groan gratitude for last fall
being rescued from floods, when gathered
industrial dryers formed a choir roaring forth
for two weeks steady in their faith in the floors
whose uncomplaining service for centuries
had earned them salvation.

Above, the choir loft dangles long philodendra
in weepy farewell, still trying to climb down from the
lofty perch the parishioners had given it.
Dutifully, it had held high their children,
imperfect cherubim, whose souls, like their coveralls,

remained soiled. The upper stained glass window
sends an amber prism of three foot wide blocks
of light in a slowly moving arc across the vaulted
white ceiling and thick walls, circling me in last embrace,
tracing a trajectory towards the open West.

Yes, the spiral staircase made me go in circles,
but the spinning inside me was my own distress
for my unemployed neighbors. I rushed up
into the tower sometimes without noticing
others had to walk in very straight paths
to find a way from day to day or out of town.

I will miss being the imported Jewish professor
living in the old Lutheran Church, finding peace
in the pews of a Pennsylvania farther from
New York City than the miles on the map,
a haven of neighbors who used to shake hands
outside on the plaza I made into a garden.

The church tower overlooks the town blocks
that line up on the banks to witness the river
meander towards a peaceful end somewhere else.
Climbing the ladder to the steeple, I listen
to the flocks of birds about me in the treetops
sing the end of the day.

Moving to California

Moving, it takes two years for the body to drift
down in the winds, skin billowing in the breeze
like a tail-whipping Chinese dragon kite.

On the way down, a wrist might surge high
in an updraft, flapping as if conducting air
symphonies on the end of an empty sleeve.

On the way down, the head also flops back
and forth, until, *smack*! It hits the ground in
the folds of a gathered epidermal parachute.

Gusts of wind streak in from the east where
the void of our absence is the eye of a storm
blowing with bent trees our past towards us.

Meals set out on the new dining table fly away
—homing pigeons, flapping back to circle our
old place like LA airplanes awaiting clearance.

When we make love, I see the Pennsylvania
clouds in your eyes as the West Coast king-size
bed squeaks like a Philadelphia trolley car.

Moving Back after Two Years in California

Only for a while will trees still vibrate for me
in flitting movements of shifting glee
like kids fitfully tearing open holiday presents,
as the trees laugh and invite me like them
to grow leafy and hang pendulously on the
Susquehanna bank, while my foot still braces
    against dry, flinty desert ground.

Only I, in this small Pennsylvania town,
hear the death of freeways, cars
finally whooshed up and away into the skies,
their drone sucked into the upper air
to give newfound silence. Afternoon
thunderheads are their ghosts trying
to pour down noise, but here
    it's humid sweet.

My neighbor sees me walk by and
scratches his head at how long
he didn't notice my walks,
not knowing of my other life,
and when we greet he thinks my grin
is from starting beers too early
in the day instead of feeling
    how very late I am

to drink in these rural days,
needing to have left here for there
in order to first arrive at where
I had been for ten years walking
these streets. Second honeymoon, I
want to hold my joy for the river
pushing relentlessly past,
    instead of commuters.

Ducks like Slanted Rain from the Sky

Twenty ducks slide the air skimming ripples
of water gray against the lighter gray spray
through which they stretch their bodies
further than they measure in the river's wake.

The current pulls them down from the sky
to seek the secret of its powerful slide
so they can ride a while on the skin of the river
rather than seek above lines of flight.

An autumn swift of flood filled waters
swerves through the banks and surges around
the once lazy curve of the snaking bend
whose waters are sent forward more quickly

with this rush of streaking surface and flying followers
who are pulled by a force that cuts its way through
the clumps of trees and hills and small towns
to the speed of emptying oneself out of the sky.

Running Under the Snow Geese

For this month of March, each year, as we jog
past clapboard faces of former inns and taverns,
homes of canal and river boat captains,
past former warehouses whose visages
are wizened with a few centuries of gazing
across the street over the running river,
it is in the sky above us a swiftly
flowing current streams.

I crane my face upwards as we make our way
down the street, pulled in several directions.
My pumping arms seem to be swallowed
by the swollen river current and I am
carried down around the wide river bend,
over the guzzling rocks and under the arches
of the stone bridge. But the force of habit
propels me forward with you through
the streets of evening.

Tonight, the strongest pull is overhead,
on the countercurrent of those crossing our path
with their honking calls and surging desire
to soar across the country, to slip inside
their well-worn way in the sky
from the bay to river to tundra,
as an urge grabs at my sneakers to streak up
into place in the stretching line of their "V."

My eyes follow above as my feet stumble ahead,
yet our steps striking the road draws me
into our wake, as the love
mingling between our panting breaths
is the compass of my journey
and my heart flaps calmly back into line with yours
as I hear the immature geese squawk
at the sunset to lead them home.

Living by the Railroad Tracks

Friends said the rumbling roar punctuating my sleep and
morning tea would disturb the orderly march of thought
from left to right and leave me looking sideways in the mirror.
Especially, they said, the long horn blast screaming away,
away from here, sounding bassoon-like if bassoonists were insane
and amplified by a woofer filling the lower sky and accompanied
by a stadium full of red-faced fiends blowing their minds out.

Perhaps, when I saw the house and the tracks running by,
I thought how dramatic to be in bed, both of us coming
to the moment of chugging explosion and really feeling
the earth move. Or I saw myself floating above the tracks
saber in hand, gleaming light flaring out at the onrushing
beast for once a knight of glory rather than a book tender.
Or maybe I knew the sound of the American frontier, oh

so very American, long sounding train thunder and wail
might make me feel as if I belonged again to this land and
as if it had a history that still made sense and could summon
me to smile in my sleep for the visions of my grandparents
crammed into the lower decks of freighters sailing to the dream
of this new life without sabers being rattled over their heads
and plunged into their hearts in a place where they didn't belong.

I like to be reminded of the constant movement and iron
pushing people into the night faster than the current in the river
beside the tracks. The flashing eyes in the woods
are the only
witnesses to the lumbering behemoths
with families in their
bellies crashing through the dark
to where the black ends,
even though the windows
are blacker yet and only reflect
swaying blank faces
before arriving at welcoming stations.

Susquehanna Floods and the Fullness of Breasts

The fullness of breasts had never seemed
really to be like the fullness of the current
until these mid-winter waters sprint through
the river valley impelled by relentless rain.

Now, I can feel the skin of the river
pucker with life's fluids full as if bursting
and lifting above the surface of the flow
while also sinking below its rush within.

The water is so high, it curves on its way
gathering in such a swell, it offers itself
as if soft against my face and also against
the light, so that to touch it is to caress it,

just as the silky bursting arc of your breasts
requires my lips to move over them in kiss,
my tongue to be swept into the circles of
round lapping within your heart's currents.

Only with the fluid meeting of land and sky
in an overflow forbidden by the normal
order of geography and weather can I now
feel the river flowing within your chest.

October Monsoon Night

Rain dives headlong onto the shingled roof
feathering the tiles in percussive runs
like bass piano notes serenading our peace
meant to accompany
quiet sighs of belonging together
in our house that sounds tonight
like a tent of care under skies of dark.

Equinox passed, the earth begins to recline
deep into its pillows of black space,
moving away from sitting warmly among us
towards its solitary rest, but having just turned away,
we still see its smile and feel the warmth of its breath
on our chests as we lie on a couch of early fall

drowsy and still reflecting summer's light
onto each other's skin, the sun in our eyes
gentles with wind and raindrops as they tap
above our heads, a reminder
we will soon have to bundle up
and sit in the closeness of heart.

A Pond behind the Susquehanna Canal House

We dug all weekend the rocks beneath
centuries of pine needles and weeds
become soil sunk deeper
since the canal men drank beer here
to stiffen their backbone
so they could stand up
to the ornery mules
that pulled coal and planks
and the men's lives on the barges
of the canals through the months
of the men aching to follow
their women across the hearth
to a bed of quilts and welcome,
to leave for a time the river's relentless push
beside the canal's endless stream—
the engines for getting the rich man's
wares to the city stores.

Two centuries later, there are
no piles of drunken men
under the trees behind the tavern,
only the zip of straight lined hummingbirds
wishing to read books on our laps
but settling for skimming the text
of red fuscia hanging over our heads,
as we march around back under the pines
to pile stones heavy with history
in a circular wall shaped
like the circles of Susquehannock
who rested here still as the pines
after paddling the river across the way—
until the Paxton boys
hired to help raise real estate prices
broke into Lancaster jail
where the last of the tribe
was being protected
and cut the circle of their lives.

We fill the pond knowing
once long ago there was another pond
in the middle of hardened lives
like the solid white ash
harder than any other tree
and so logged to extinction,
floated down the river to far off places
to make sturdier houses around the world
and perhaps even this public house,
but here, there has always been rest,
a pond for the weary movers
and the pursued to sit and see the sky
in the middle of a circle of pines,
a blue-faced mirror of something higher,
above mules, the glut of logs and bounty hunters,
a gathering of softly sewn heron flights
and the meander of the current
pooled in the cupped palms of stones
offering a silent psalm of still water.

Silently, we place the stones
above ground where they were buried
for ages of neglect and form a fence
in a new circle, hoping to mend
the centuries of broken ones
and dance a slow dance with the spirits
still sleeping within the centuries of needles.
We know they would be pleased
they built a path whose curving closure
in its wider circle contains for us
enough time to watch lazy goldfish
find poetic inspiration in the pond
tracing undulating sketches through the water
as if Matisse were released from his body
and his flowing hands given fins and scales
to swim his sinuous line for us all day
weaving around us a spell
of softly turning water grace.
The hummingbirds know
in whirring above us
that we too sip a nectar,
but ours is culled
from those still present
at this canal lock of repose.

Wood Pile Love Song

The thunk, thunk of each log
tossed on the pile sounds a note
in thumping its way into
the right shaped crevice—
a thrill like finding my way into you—
where it belongs—and I belong,
resounding behind the house
in an autumn bass on bass song
of fitting in with the earth and you.

Chopped wood sides against each other
form cross-hatched spaces
of interlocked triangles
that seem to make a hollow face
of wizened contemplation
that smiles in the cool sun
to encourage me
to roll in the leaves
and remember how our parts
even at angles form an oaken mosaic
where pieces hold together
in enormous strength
despite the odd shaped spaces
and the whole rounded, tilting pile
stands resting in exquisite balance.

II. The Past Is Lost

The Extinction of the Tall Tale

In these days when hard data rules,
there is no room for the Tall Tale:
lives so deeply imagined and cherished,
they blossom without seeds
ever having been sown
in the soil of facts
we now obsessively sift.

It is clearly criminal
to embroider a colorful past
when all is black or white,
one or zero:
the morality of correct sums
and predictable lives.

Barber shops are raided,
boots kick in coffee klatch doors,
bathroom stalls are repainted,
and the past is photographed.

The hum of silicon vigilance
replaces the burble of the story:
The grown men who became boys
repeating endless war yarns,
like rondos with cascading refrains,
are quiet with proper regard
for facts and figures.

No more do we listen with respect
to how Jack lifted the log
from the frightened kids,
how Gertrude baked Lysol
in the town's brownies, or
how George wrote the great novel
before he left it on his towel,
while in the dunes
with the Jersey beach queen,
too busy to notice the incoming tide.

So many heroes with erect shoulders,
so many events with pop corn drama,
so many visitors from other galaxies,
are herded into dungeons
with rats for company,
the invisible millions
that Antiseptic Thought hopes
drowned down there
with the strychnine of precision,
but the rodents and the sagas
rule the subways of the soul.

Arroyo Seco Canyon Restaurant Dog

The pale blue eyes
have been here before,
when these hills
had winds sweeping clean
flights down into the valley.
The eye of the wolf
part of the wind,
not an obstruction like
this bright green tinned roof chalet
stuck into the slope
to become the eye overlooking
and yet not part of,
sage strewn rocky
washes skipping down.

Sprawled across the doorway
wolf and dog having become one
in the progress from rushing wind
to this barbecue steakhouse,
watching with eyes
so white-blue pale
they are the fringe
where sky and cloud blur,
opening another sky
within the sky,
the hazy hole
where time gets caught
floating over and over
becoming entwined
in its own wispy strands.

The dog's eye has within its swirling
an innocent place of wolves
soaring in the wind
no one will ever find.
I look lost in these mirrors,
imperturbable yet wild,
eyes of wolf, shepherd, and husky,
and slide by ice fields,
howling wind-whipped
tree limbs, skipping spirits
down the slopes
straining at the trunks
to join the rush
down into the mad swirl
of baying, blowing abandon,
now sitting quietly on a doormat.

Alzheimer's Railway Conductor

He stood, railway cap askew, in the doorway of his hospital room,
arm rising with his voice to exclaim, "Next station is Back Bay."
Around him, people laughed and couldn't see into his gloom.

Or perhaps they saw better, for on these tracks he didn't see his doom.
The scuffles and groans of the ward were like passengers on any day
he stood, railway cap askew, in the doorway of his hospital room.

The light from the faces that reflected into his were always the loom
upon which he wove his own life story from what they would say.
Around him, people laughed and couldn't see into his gloom.

Now we tried to help him remember he was trying to eat, to groom,
to shit, but found no light in his eye, the never-ending train—only ray,
he stood, railway cap askew, in the doorway of his hospital room.

He marveled at the passengers, the woman with the hat with a plume
who sat on his lap, while he grinned guiltily and said he couldn't pay.
Around him, people laughed and couldn't see into his gloom.

She told him it was on her, for forty years he'd known her womb.
Be careful of my wife, he warns, as he takes his wife as his newest lay.
He stood, railway cap askew, in the doorway of his hospital room,
around him, people laughed and couldn't see into his gloom.

How the Word Lost its Voice

In the beginning, there was the word,
a modest sign pointing toward
where silence had its ground.
Then, so many uses were found.

First words were cut to be clothing.
Their stylish patterns hid our loathing,
words hemmed for the occasion
to appear muted and never brazen.

When words began to be dropped from the skies,
no one knew what was in disguise,
what was buried under a phrase,
so many words, they created a haze.

At one point, the word took to the cross:
"I am the way to find your loss,
I am the way back to the place
where silence is the master of all space."

But the word never finished,
with so many, each turn was diminished.
"I am the way" was all that was heard:
silence forgotten, they worshipped the word.

When silence could no longer be found,
when words covered every inch of ground.
silence was known as lack of the word.
Its song was lost, no longer to be heard.

The Famous Artificial Heart Experiment

There were no boundaries for him
once they removed his heart.
The bedside lamp broiled his liver
with its scalding light, the chill
draft running across the hospital floor
went straight to his tongue—
it froze in mid-sentence waggle—
and the nurse's hips
crushed his squeaking lobes,
surrounding them with their fleshy elegance.

Tied by throbbing hoses
to the clanking Jarvik Seven,
he was propelled relentlessly into space,
pushed assertively further
since his blood no longer
danced with the moon,
but was driven by metallic fanaticism.
The beats hammered at his mind
until holes opened
and he leaked away.

The doctors had feared
his senses would become too mechanical
paced by a cast iron pump,
after the pulpy center was removed.
How his thoughts got dispersed
was a puzzle, since clever with gears
and tubes, they never felt how we think
from the body's rhythmic kinship
with all that beats around it,
in time with clouds scudding skyward,
the bobbing of flowers on their stalks,
and even the ebb and flow of traffic:
the way the beating of the world
beats out its time in our hearts,
and so in our heads.

There is an ancient ability
of cells to listen
while pumping, to receive
in the midst of pushing,
that allows the world
to herd our feelings,
like wayward cattle,
into the corral of who we are.

Cyberspace Theology

Aphrodite lurks somewhere in the sites of the internet. If
we seek the root directory, all the goddesses can be found,

dancing around the labyrinthine algorithm that generates
perfect bodies and transparent minds. The gods are there,

too, riding search engines on heroic quests. We want our
will translated into binary values. All the ones, we will add

up, but delete the zeroes. Some build fortunes through post-
modern pixel castles in the air, money made truly from

nothing. We no longer believe in heaven above earthly space
or in infinite mercy, so we seek salvation in more megabytes,

from e-mails from the furthest reaches, and maybe beyond,
counting files instead of sins, and cleanse not our souls, but

our hard drives. Cyberspace exists nowhere within real time
or space—the same location where the old heaven was supposed

to be. Its revelation is no burning bush or walking on water,
since these feats are only beginner's level on our kids' video

games. We no longer want a higher reality. We'd rather gossip
in Plato's cave of moving shadows and winking virtuality.

Deprivation Tournament

Like stickball or poker,
   who had it worse
can be played for hours
   when a sudden streak
enlivens the circle
   but doesn't mean defeat.

In their seventies,
   she explains, it's glorious
at night,
   in the gathering dark
to pitch your childhood woes
   onto the table

making the hard times
   a winning suit,
redeeming old pains
   stuck in your bones
with story gold
   of added palliative elements

all can play
   with a bankroll of groans
and a wishful turning themselves
   round into characters
an old pro, she leans back
   into mid-game stride

rending the air with a gasp
   of having one pair of sneakers
for two little girls, sisters
   switching shoes in hallways before gym
or going to the pool every other day
   wishing the suit yours on the hotter;

warming up, she tells of blankets so heavy
    in the caboose of the railroad flat
they had to be lifted off by adults
    or children remain forever in quilted purgatory;
like winter wolves surrounding a lone rabbit,
    we see seven children around one package of jello;

every week the silent cinema would resound
    with smashed tinkling plates on the floor
when patrons packed the hall for "dish night"
    but forgot their bounty when lost in screen kiss,
and the sticky sweet clouds of tangerine vapors
    would rise from the kids only packed treat;

the gypsies had to live in storefronts
    feared in apartments they'd steal children away,
but her brother wrote to Aldous Huxley
    who flew him to California to pal around
with Christopher Isherwood, around pools,
    where they all had their own bathing trunks.

Warming up for young people can hurt, and
    can strain the arm, throwing too hard.
With the other old-timers, the pains are batted
    quickly out of the park where they sit,
and then the words don't linger long enough
    to hear how in them the dead speak and cry.

Babi Yar

For the 30,000 Jews machine-gunned by the Nazis, 9/29/41

They could not know
what they were doing at Babi Yar,
a hand cannot not know this,
the bodies sailing off the ledge,
flesh reflecting sun a last time.

Wide mouths stretch open,
gliding holes of disbelief,
their cries a torn parachute
as they plunge stiff into a pit
where each falls into gears
of a wheel jerkily turned.

Nothing planted in this ditch
to grow
as bobbing the corpses
rise in our throats
when we start to speak the
names of those
whose end was compost.

A Generation of Boys Who Love Terror

With rabid fury, as if the fenders were wagging,
—and not a slippery, black, distended tongue—
the gleaming eyes of death are not a suffering dog's
but rather belong to the driver's glassy stare,
inflamed with the nuclear virus of martyrs,
as he drives his explosive truck
at the concrete temple's doors.
For him, he's entering Leviathan's belly
with jostling visions of burnt, mangled flesh.
The borrowed, miniaturized technological might,
wired by the will of God, angry at short-circuits,
has infected a generation of boys
with terminal glory fever.

The slap to all his faces,
God will have to endure,
imprisoned with us within technology,
and spilled across seas in oil slicks
poured like holy wine in His Name,
and lost amidst the roar of plastic explosives
replacing the silence of prayer—
boys everywhere jacketed in bombs
the new church vestments.
They call for His blessing:
"we will be your devils,
casting out your imperfect creations,
and give you an empty world
to try again, if you will help us find
love's blaze in the acetylene purity
in the sacrament of the bomb."

The mantra of the electric god
charges the global lines, so the good
word spreads of these newest
testament boys at play.

September Eleventh of a New Millennium

This glide from the sky has none of the grace
of birds wheeling in flight or leaves breezily spinning,
even though we often see planes that way,
this straight-line trajectory is fueled by hate
and rather than alighting in a nest of care,
it strikes through the heart of humanity.

Like the image of bullets striking the head of
Kennedy, we will dream fitfully at night of
planes exploding glass and flame in two towers
that fall with the same dead weight of violence
as a young President toppled backwards into his
limousine. Like dominoes, they are trying

to make us topple, too, into our nightmare
of an eye for an eye. We will fall headlong,
being pushed so, for there is no other way but
down, yet, it could be into the arms of others
where we open our eyes to their bright glance.

The Appalachian Space of this Eternal Return

There's not much to say when eight hundred
miles are not enough space,
when asked to leave
since the ghosts have taken all
the room in your house and heart.
You patiently explain you will call
when the dead have died again,
but not in time for Valentine's Day.

I could say that we dream of infinity,
broken-crested to see the same
humble kitchen table, formica,
with nicks and yellow varicose veins,
that because we made love
protected within the bower of your hair
for a month straight, always
looking eye to eye, simultaneously
dizzy with jazz notes pianoed from Germany.

You would say that's not relevant
that you must send your skin
out to be dry-cleaned,
that you need the stratosphere,
but it is the soil of Appalachia
that buries its women
unmarked, that presses:
a woman too who can't be buried.

A broken collarbone
keeps you picking up wounded birds,
gift of a schizophrenia-eyed mother.
For her, it was a furious mountain chore
like chopping wood.
It saved the men the effort:
from the line of broken collarbones
came the dice the men roll at night.

You will never get that far
that the snap of your bones is unheard.
It buzzes after you like a berserk bee

and stings and stings,
and whenever a hand goes to touch you
for an uncertain instant
the collarbone will always cry,
the heart beneath it will flutter.

The Gravity that Pulls Us through the Floor

There is a gravity that pulls us down relentlessly
even though we think it stops at the ground
or at the floor or when our chin hits the table
or the downward toe stubs the rock. But it
never stops pulling and pulling, even if we
were to land amazed at the earth's exact center.

For the gravity whose limits we can reach
is the one Einstein pinned down in newfangled
equations. It didn't like to be pinned down the
way it does to us and sought revenge. In a mind-
blowing century it let itself to be torn apart to
tear bigger holes in our flimsy world. Hiroshima

and Nagasaki were the big shows, but it also
let hot elements keep coming apart and sneak
into our cells to do them in from the inside out.
Even unprovoked, it pulls at our things to break
and causes us to cry in pain that we are stuck
in the somewhere we don't want to be.

The other gravity, however, pulls us right through
the floors of those we love, to keep us gliding
down with arms and legs spread to land in
strange beds entwined with others, the baffled
heart still resting on the upper floors, where it
thought it was safe at home. As we are happy

to be happy as the years pass, it looks for a
small crack in our fidelity, a more perfectly
rounded ass or a flatter stomach, a more ardent
member with greater staying power,
a bearer of flowers or someone who will listen
with eyes focused on the nuances, through
which it can tear through a hole in the bedroom
or den and suck us below into black caves of
free-fall where others wait with lit candles
and new illusions. This is the gravity of weariness
that slows the pumping of our interest in our
obsessions, the job landed but who cares now

for the later success sought decades before,
the great reviews, the big vista, the walk in
space, by the body that no longer
believes in what it took to get here. When
we lose our hands that shaped our caresses
we have arrived at this gravity's source.

The Lost Fossil Fuel of Passion

How do you come to register
the sudden missing degree of heat,
hear the pause flag between the notes,
even though it's an improvised chord?

The rocking and rocking,
head on breast
still soothes away a cruel world,
but the motion lulls,
like an ocean cruise,
instead of tearing the sky.

Can the veins of glinty ore
catch the eye of the prospector
bent like his mule,
both grinding their teeth,
with tongue still licking friendly,
but almost catching a finger
with too long laboring angry?

To feel the new in the old
is a fossil wisdom
of dark tubbing feet
ceremonially splayed,
paint on rock walls inviting
crickets to hop into the song,
around the fires dancing.

But the modern foot
feeling through concrete
the refreshing pool
within the thick muddy
tall grass meadows cemented underneath
walks calmly past
the magic circle of masks
not realizing their straw tongues
can breathe fire,
or that we two could again
become apes of passion.

Morning Memories

To sleep without dreams
is no brain failure or
lazy chemicals having lost their ion tails,
no longer attractive to their mates.

To sleep without dreams
is to have forgotten the touch
of fire on your back, or how
your quirks were a labyrinth of wonder

for some other, sure your history
had undiscovered artifacts
of gasping beauty and hidden languages
with secrets of desire and hope;

you were important in the unfolding
of the cosmos, and it was silly,
but so sweet, like pomegranate seeds
slipping out of your hands and

skipping into the imagination,
where sugared waters attracted
deep-night hummingbirds
whirring visions.

III. To the Edge of Return

When the Doctor Said Cancer

The sky becomes a revolving door whooshing
madly as the clouds pour through jostling by.
Shoulder to shoulder, they rush out from some
crack in the mid-heavens where the answers are.
Grabbing at them, I am whirled around and aloft
since the weight of my body is gone, already a ghost.

Days later, I fall towards an earth that has lost
its sun. People are unaware there is no light
in a total eclipse. The streets are flooded
even though cars drive on. Accountants check
figures, yet no one registers the work. All chairs
are empty, filled only by puffs of an acrid steam,
as if they were residues of some former life.

In another moment, workers move on silently,
bobbing after one another, like lines of gulls
who chase scraps at the shore, as if it had
never happened. Each few minutes, they all
suddenly collapse. From the point in the sky
all the clouds come tumbling out again
and weep in a circle. The floods and the
darkness, the onrush and the sudden calm
must frighten them. It is clumsy watching
the daily news after the world is gone.

A Week after Colon Cancer Stage IV Discovered

     I pin your scoped image on the wall
         like in the team's locker room   enemy
           to be defeated
  enmity   you or me
      this time, it's the whole game

      the tumor has a blind face   like some moving
black hole   that can only devour
  like the timing of ticks   marching in my gut
     looking the same sickening green yellow black
of a sky before the twister,   but its colors are in me

only in this decade   can I have the cancer's
    portrait leering at me
         visage of a psycho
    who wants   to give me a kick me in the gut
  or looks like   a ragtag of homeless cells
      seeking a meal.

Dale lost her breasts and she was wild   for   years
    for a touch,   a man,   a high
    lifting soar into the
place she was afraid they cut out of her
     and that all of us bastards would deny her

  and she was scared
     when
      the bleeding drains
 protruding from her scarred chest
     turned them on

                    I understand the perverse now
                I have to hate these dumb cells
                        and love the quiet humming
                    of the techno-gadget haven of
radioactively efficient   destruction   care
                            they offer me

I need the power over nature
            I have loved so delicately
        but now must detest   as   invading me
    it   deserves the napalm   they'll shoot inside me
                to burn its heart out
      before mine is gone.

Nothing to Say

The brain tumor,
like a cap fitted carefully
inside another cap,
instead of lining the mind
with woolen security,
takes the space where
your thoughts used to be.
Its tentacles reach down to grab
words from your sentences,
so each line's a metaphor
unappreciated by the cashier
and bus driver who can't fathom
the sudden, poetic inspiration.

It takes your tongue by surprise
as we both look at the gaps
and into each other's eyes,
as if the missing words
would run across your corneas
like the Times Square bulletins,
as you squint
and put a finger carefully
along the side of your forehead
for ideas that are gone,
and I look away
from the falling fruit
that fills your eyes.

Caught Suddenly Dying in a Dream

We think always of the moment of
death come to face us as the inevitable
visit of the one at the bedside who
glares soundlessly, without a face,
who takes up no space before us,

as if blackness absorbed into itself
all its blackness, and we wordless
look beyond vision to a point
suspended in the air where
all the air leaks out of itself
and we float into the void.

Yet, we might miss the only
certain encounter of our lives,
if caught in sleep, adrift
in the air of the night,
this visitor sneaks to our bed
and flies behind our eyes to

take us in dream, and then
blackness bursts forth from
itself searing yellows and laughing
blues in the hall of dreams,
the sudden swirl of hues

spirals down a never-ending
drain to drag us along with them,
into the middle of the pinwheel
where there is no pinwheel,
spinning, forever spinning,

no morning to come
nor farewells to be said,
just a corpse on a bed
with a hurricane inside
whose eye will never open.

Six Days Sailing toward the Moon

I

The Purple Possum Band tosses notes of brass
and trumpet into the early Saturday morning shafts of light,
making the air burst with a spectral confetti of tones
as we row with the beat over the bay in our dinghy,
paddling to make land a slipping memory.

We joke at the town's feting our launch, but know
down deep where the flounder lie on the bottom,
the celebration is not for us, but for August and
the discovery of light. We head towards the sails
beyond the rocks and the floor of foam hoping
we will learn to blow music from our chests.

II

At night, the skipper groans as he crawls around
his bunk, a crab, scuffling for a future.

In the morning, stolid like the birds atop the pilings,
he tells us how his wife sent him off with a dirge,

divorce or else, nineteen years overboard.
We make coffee in reply and feel the wind enter us.

III

Approaching Hell's Kitchen, the boat chucked in to boil,
we feel dizzy with a hundred cauldrons around us.
We flee the barge tailgating like ten fourteen-wheelers
tied together and set afloat to monster our path.
About to be run over from behind, where doom
always comes from, at the last instant it glides
to the side—dead, as if losing intent or beheaded
by some unseen marine knight of the pass.

IV

The captain declares we are not crew
but passengers, not worthy of our keep.
Even so, in the cabin bunk we become mates,
and find among waves, currents
lost since childhood. Running on deck
with new charts, we turn the helm towards
a course unknown to the skipper.
These are waters that allow the rock
in his stomach to dissolve into the sea.

V

In the creak of the hawsers, I hear dead friends.
Their souls escape gulls who have an eye
only for fish. The smiles of the dolphins

on the Jersey coast are not for them, nor do buoys
mark their graves. Only the relentless slap on the bow
seems a reminder of how they once swam and sank.

Their memories are the swells that upset
my sleep below in the bunk. Going on deck,
I peer into the black for their wake.

Sailing toward the Light

Your last sail still sought the sun
following its path through the waves,
a trail marked by golden leaves of light
left for a moment to mark the way
through the shifting blue dance of water
before they begin to disperse
dropped by a great thoughtless hand
we never get to see
tracing the course you had to take.

You were five years old
clutching a tiller in pursuit of the path
when you first started to chase
the sun, told by stubbly chin
old sailors to get out on the water
to drown what ailed you
and to begin the sail
in the sun's wake
to the point where it leaps into the sky.

Your life always leaned over into the roil
of a line across the sea
where you were most yourself
smiling at the helm in tracing
a disappearing line
that traverses a life, pursued
through the choppy history
of the calms and storms
that never blemish the maps
with their temporary fury and release
but still go deep enough to inscribe themselves
upon the softer matter of our souls.

You wrote a novel entitled chasing
the sun, but most never saw
the pools of water
around your feet, how the land
was a lie for you with its shutters and roofs
that shielded us from the glint
of the daily trek
across the ocean above us
reflected in the waves
of the other sea below
whose end was your constant destination.
A week before your heart stopped
at the helm in the lee of the sun,
a day ending in the wash of
a little island still afloat
from within your childhood,
you told your daughter
that your religion was the sea
and the way it spread across
the horizon moving endlessly
towards the fading light of day,
and I must imagine
that you squinted one last time
in seeing its gleaming wake
disappear into the coming night.

The Asymptote of Loss

Knowing we are all time and space doesn't soothe
when the slapping of your unsteady feet upon the floor
seems like a slower rendition of Taps
even though I try to appreciate each halting step
as a declaration we still walk the same earth.
Soon your new path will be all angles to mine,
upon the other earth which seems like
it might be only inches away
hidden behind blowing tree branches
or beneath the river's racing waters
or within streaking clouds in the west,
somewhere silky nearby,
that is infinitely distant,
even beyond
love's power to birth matter.

On good days, I know we can't lose those we love
since time is a pool of light in which we swim
and the dead are stealthy shining columns
who slip into the sunlight,
offering themselves
to fire our vision,
and add a warmth that not only surrounds us
but also emerges from within us.
Despite this, it will seem dark
when those I love skip
into a roundabout of radiance
whose spectrum of colors
is beyond my vision.

Full Body Pet Scan

I

The two heads of the nurses swivel in
military precision as they mark seconds
on the hospital clock of how long
the radioactive genie is loose in the room
before being siphoned into my veins.
The lead lid is lifted slowly to release
the racing half-life to be shot within me
to measure what of my struggling life
is left. The deadly dye will tempt the cells
of death out of hiding to gorge themselves
in confusion, since like absorbs like,
disorder into disorder.

II

For the particles to dance freely through
my cell walls, I must sit absolutely still
in the test room as if in a cell with no
space or interest except to offer ravenous
nuclei a chance to sink their teeth into my
inner core. Straps across my forehead,
chest and legs bind me to a board in the scanner.
I am the bait in a mousetrap waiting for
the cancer to make a false move and be seen.
Instead of spreading rat poison on the garage
floor, they've put it in my veins enticing
the damned parasites' hunger with a dying
heavy metal whose fleeting life will be gone
in a hundred and ten minutes while
the cancer seeks eternity over me.

III

Instead of becoming inert in waiting for
the frenzied radioactive span of decay to
end, I resonate to the shouted words
of my friend reading book reviews down
the scanning tunnel. He hoots with each
criticism of mine he knows I would make
if not sworn to be a mummy and lays it
on thick to accentuate every pompous
phrase in the famous intellectual review.
He never comments on the straps, the
glistening, shrieking machinery, or about
the half-lives exploding away within me.
Now, when I think of sliding through
some final celestial scanner, worrying where
we are headed, I imagine angels of mercy
never mentioning our sordid lives and
reading in a choir book reviews.

Preoperative Sutra

As they wheeled my cart forward,
it splashed onto the banks of the Ganges,
a place that I'd never been, but where
I had sat cross-legged for centuries.

The river mist was permeated with
shadows chanting, a faithful chorus
of orange-clad monks singing for me
a path into the operating room.

Decades ago, when a confused student
had sat on a zafu, they had seen me
across this river through the span of
thousands of years counting breaths.

Never did I feel their patient eyes upon me
until I slid into the moving waters that morning.
Form is emptiness, emptiness is form
filled the oxygen they pumped into me.

The nurses and the techs joked with me
as I laughed at the Bodhisattva's resounding
words of how there is no tongue, body
or mind, no thought or cease of thought.

On the operating table, I became a large
slithering fish whose strong strokes
had lost its river. There is no pain
nor cease from pain intoned the monks.

The gleaming medical machines had
all become unlikely rocks and shoals
slowing down the current of emptiness
rushing towards the falls ahead.

No fear of cancer nor loss of colon
nor liver seemed to be the next line
of the sutra, as the smiling Boddhisattva
said gone, gone, way beyond, gone.

To the Edge

The bottom was last Memorial Day,
not remembering the war dead,
since it was my death,
accompanied by loved ones,
who seemed to pace the cages
of the Philadelphia Zoo,
as a week before surgery,
as we tried to kill time
on the day of the dead
by looking at living creatures.

I stared at cages and felt my soul pace
with tigers, sink into the ooze with hippos,
dully chew on hay with the stupefied gorilla
and rattle against the bars of a thirty percent
chance to live five years. Each person
at the zoo that day seemed caged
in bars tighter than those around the animals.
They would live and I would die
and they didn't know they were alive
in the sun without confinement
of a death sentence.
Please, let me slap each of them
to feed them kernels of recognition.

It was a day of following after death
on the way from life to the edge.
As I looked over, she held me by my belt
as I almost slipped into the dark.
The next morning, in bed,
yesterday's hole in my hope
seemed more like a circular moat
to keep me safe within my kin.
An island of peace within an oasis
of soft whisper
and preserved animals of grace
against the poachers of joy
and the tamers of life.

IV. Futures to Reawaken the Past

The Last Train to the Heart

The last train to the heart brims with clanking cars,
makes shrill squeaks that echo at the sharp bends,
but rolls heavily forward, reluctant to stop or slow
with its momentum of freight on board.
Then, it descends more carefully all the way down,
arriving at the inner stockyards of soul
surrounded with pens and fences
built during snows and years of hard work
against storms of disappointment.

The train was long expected, decades overdue,
the sidings for acceptance finally finished and painted
a resilient copper hue, flecked with hopeful blue stars.
The looping track guides the obedient cars
in a circle around the heart, as they glide
with the engine off, gradually slowing
and shifting their path into
quiet meditation,
as the boys of childhood
arriving on former voyages
wave from the windows,
as friends and relatives munch hay on flatbeds
and coal is packed away
into boxcars of memory
to fire the engine of transformation.

The Body of the Dark

The body of the dark is not evil
as it grows from buried things,
cousin to autumnal blackened stalks
and ferns of somber thought,
absorbing light and laughter
becoming hard carbon
standing in midst of gardens
like sentinels perseverating
we have lessons to learn
and a past to make right
when old pains
calcify stems.

The body of the dark
is no enemy, yet
distrusted, its mien remains
impassive,
silently offering
insistent weight,
a solid mantra
that offers us
hurt into recognition,
while confetti selves
impressing others
are blown away.

The body of the dark
shows us the right to heft,
in the evening's gloom
it glows darkly
like an ember
of persistent memory,
like a loon flying through the night
but spying its lake,
like an onyx sculpture
whose every crevice
seems to trace soul.

Poor Boys, Rare Tortoises, and Existential Choices

Once, I spent many months discussing if we
should save turtles who cross roads in springtime,
mad with the urge to mate, launching themselves
into asphalt galaxies of speeding metal gargantuans,
who squash these erotic flights under their tires.
Since each creature needs to fulfill its karma,
Buddhist compassion tells us to let it go.
To respect existential choice is to respect
terrapin resolve like the resolve of any.
Failing as philosophers, we stopped our cars
to rush into the road to save turtles.

Now, the little boy runs up to me with a box
held to his chest at the spot on my run
where I pass his place, the row of old forge houses.
In his box is an infant tortoise, not the snake
or rat or box turtle I expected, but a very quiet
visitor from some finer landscape than our river
factory town. From my student days, I recognize
its face and shell of perfectly fluted rising pyramids,
with bowed legs curving like a ballerina at the barre,
from a shop in another poor, river town with pets
priced for easy sale, except the miniature tortoise,
who seemed to hear vibrations of other spheres
and walked as if he could remember a royal clamor.

He had traveled far, a captive of fates
more pitiless than those tormenting Odysseus,
and I knew he had somewhere his own realm
with a Penelope waiting. I had wanted to buy
his freedom, until that day he was stolen.
Decades later, halted on my run, I looked
into the boy's box, thought of fear and choice,
tortoises and rare kingdoms, and ran on.
Perhaps, I had learned to respect the mad dash
or small prisons of karma, whether of friends
or rare tortoises captured by thoughtless boys,
or perhaps I had finally become a philosopher.

Van Gogh at Arles

The dread secret of light
burned the hands beyond recognition,
made trees of paint—
twisting their hues
until they blossomed
with courtesans against the sky.
Pigments blew in the wind
so a dark song of noon and searing night
became the green fire blazing
inside the eyelids, closed
but still burning.
Alizarins snaked through the field,
hissed in the flowers,
piled high atop each other in the gardens—
a mass of eels, thick and twisting,
maddened by the glare.

A fit of black to stop.
Yet, to go out again into the burning color!
But why not just purple in a cafe glass?
Why be singed again—
irises scarred by spitting hues—
so surrounded by pigmented branches,
lost in their thicket?
But the secret must yield, and
the colors wave
with mercy,
as fellow sufferers signaling
they too are the slaves of light.

Van Gogh at St. Remy

There is no asylum from the light;
there is no sanity in color,
incurable the way the brush
shakes the man. Only the painter
can see himself furtive at corridor's end,
knows even the trees outside cry
and the olive trees are epileptic.
The cypress racked by a fit
echoes a deranged sky.
The stars are beads of sweat
on a brow only the painter
tries to soothe—
paint compresses for a celestial fever.
The empty rose bushes
in a garden, cornered
with empty benches askew
point their blinded faces
towards the lightening
that crushed the pine trunk,
still rising arrogantly
in protest of asylum.

Monet's Water Lilies of Paris

Each stroke was equal
in time and will
to the hand darting forth
to pick a blossom
or push the rivulets into pools
or spread the angel's mirror on the water.

As Monet brushed his way through
hundreds of feet of canvas,
the brush strokes came to outnumber the corpses
in the trenches and the fields of France and Germany,
and in all the landscapes the painters of Europe
had thought to populate with odalisques,
before the curving female breasts were replaced
by severed limbs.
These enveloping yards of canvas,
of water veined with color flowing,
circling and skipping,
like Matisse's dancers entwining under the cobalt sky,
Monet declared to be his bouquet of flowers
for France to celebrate the peace.
He began on the day the charging soldiers stopped,
and skipping hand in hand began again.

Like a lover who insists the flowers must have a vase
as special as marking the occasion of love,
Monet insisted the large circular rooms
be built for his yards of lilies, water, and color,
so each viewing becomes a special occasion
marking love for peace,
and the steps taken for each hue,
walking round the canvases,
become a dance,
round and round,
under the open blue again.

The Loneliness of Book Writing

Whenever I've gone to the wilderness before
on long treks or to explore unholy places,
others anxiously watched for signs
that I was in shape or made it to checkpoints.

Backpacking 13 miles over the Continental Divide
I knew a ranger would find me fallen or collapsed,
or driving cross-country, my friends would expect calls
when too many states had flashed by the windshield.

Even climbing to Lobo Peak in monsoon season
a week after someone died—the afternoon rumblers
having lashed him with the white whip of electric wrath
while he clung to the only boulder up there—

my Chihuahua might make it back down the trail,
small legs on a mission so we can share
our pillow at night or someone might notice
the vultures' vortex lifting my soul into the sky.

Yet, writing a book, deep in the back country,
walking, walking, falling, breaking bones
and bruising terribly, no one seems to notice
I'm gone or even fathom there's a deadly trip

through scorpions of doubts, which sting late
in the day, when too few pages have been spread
around the desk on the floor for them to burrow into.
Water canteens are essential: when you have to start

the flow, there's no runoff. The fellow travelers
whom you find even in the Himalayas are not
out here, beneath the skies of words
or walking trails where the syntax might fail.

But worst of all are long days when all ideas
go whooshing into the vacuum which leaves me on
a space walk with the ship drifting away
since I'm the only pilot, as well as the repair crew.

I see the earth far away and looking luscious
in blue and green, but without more chapters,
there's no chance for a safe re-entry and another
flaming author flashes across the night sky.

The Ancient Root

Still by the sea, I sit and stare
at the seaweed skeleton
of a dancing underwater dream
wrenched out of its depths,
shriveled and torn,
yearning for its original step.

Its breathing green face, shimmering,
is all that remains
of that first creative movement.
The journey to this beach,
a fitful, turgid swirling
in the grasp of bitter tides
was not a noble voyage of realization,
but the long funeral slide
of a life torn from its source.

Surround me and stare
with your green faces
at my own twisting dance.
I refuse
to be wrenched
from my root in that growth
older than earth or spirit.
I seek always my root,
while others stumble
on this windblown ground—
looking into air for heavens—
they're leaves, torn loose,
and falling toward their
cold echoes.

I sit here—
quiet by the waves,
quiet on the cold sands,
quiet in my breath—
and wait to become again
the ancient root
from whose split skin
the look, shudder and cry
first came.

Pelicans at South Laguna Beach

A pelican sifts air slowly
quietly stowing it below
where wake and wind
become a gentle stream
as the air pushed astern
pools around my cheeks
and brushes the sun adrift.

Stone dead, the bird drops
through the mirror face
shattering the silvery swell
for just a turning heavy wing
second before the rush
ashore leaves behind
an eerie silent spot.

The weighty body from the sky
moves below in watery search
as centuries seem to pass
and a mournful sigh
hovers over an empty place,
as if dignity has been lost
to the rolling roils, yet a
resurrection is certain.

The Alchemical Secret of Movement

Zeno, master in his universe of logic, proved
that the inspired sprinter, making up half
the distance per measure of elapsed time,
would never catch the meandering tortoise,
for making up half of anything endlessly,
never makes it. The thinker's glory was another
case of right answer, but for wrong reasons,
of a blinding quick deduction encased in
the amber of pure reason.

If Zeno had let the turtle race the athlete
across the agora, instead of through his
mind, he would have discovered that moving
is not about a change of place. The glistening
body of Achilles would shatter the philosopher's
tidily arranged mental units in a blur of earth
and sky funneled through his heart into his
feet. Achilles would reach the marble columns
first but still not be moving as fast as the wise
terrapin. Its slow steps match its knowledge
that movement is more subtle than pumping
limbs. With more careful thought, the tortoise
knows that to remain who or what we are even
if we happen to be passing quickly through
a piece of space is still to be stuck in the
same spot as the world whizzes by.

Whereas, to truly move is to find the new
inside the old, to wake up in a different
galaxy, even if still in the same room.
A true destination slips into the blood,
so fire in the veins burns a new shape
for the outside by expanding from within.
It's an insinuation by vibration from kiss
or caress, from the rhythm of tree branches
as they sway or within the gray blue speckling
of a rock. In the deep viscera where we
really live suddenly a shift occurs that
makes me be you or also the brown robed
monk rapt in prayer. A voyage of eons
has occurred between the moment
I looked at you in hate and
I looked at you in love.

San Juan Capistrano Mission

Haze clings to the early morning ground here,
inches above its thirsty face, a seeming
shimmer of orange and brown consciousness
that slowly swirls waiting to lap up
any water that trickles across
the sandy cheek below. The packed dirt
stares up at the blanker face of the sky
—clear of any disturbances to its complexion
like all the perfect faces in Orange County—
and distrusts its look, like lovers gazing
into each other's eyes when they've come
to see the lack of celebration
in the hues of the iris.

The bougainvillea ignore the standoff,
as if ground and sky were parents
too busy arguing to feed the kids.
The bougainvillea run away, all along
the fences and the sides of aqueducts.
The exertion, without having drunk their fill,
makes them bleed wild apricot and magenta,
but they'd rather suffer color than plead
for a share from the trickle sluicing below.
They seem gaily colored Buddhist monks
who are able to climb peacefully
into themselves
rather than suffer from craving.

The neighbors on our block
have also learned the humility
of living with aridity.
We know a stream used to flow
where the blacktop of our street lies,
and the mason's furnaces for ceramics
were cooled with its waters.
Buried deep in my backyard is a clay oven
filled with jars and pots as dry as fossils.
The tiles baked in the blasting ovens
became the hands
of the Mission able to hold
the faithful in the desert.

The Natural Power of Memory

The Clark's Nutcracker knows where every seed
is stored in tree burrows and beneath wedged rock outcrops,
thousands and thousands of them
as if they were the words of an immense novel
and each one linked with the others to tell a hopeful story
that in reading and rereading,
paying attention to the tale,
it can survive the harsh months of blank windswept grounds
where no comforting messages can be discerned
flying above.

It's a hidden hieroglyphic of an old avian myth
to get through winters
that each bird writes in thistles and seeds
to leave its own Ariadne's thread
through swaying evergreens and crackling pines.
It's an unfinished composition of wings and beaks
through generations of hatchlings
knowing the Braille of the land
and the grammar of the sky
and the perfect pitch of the seasons
that only a Homer, Tolstoy or Beethoven
can leave for us secreted
in the midst of our winter.

The Other Time of Encounter

The slivers of time's soul
are said by scientists to waft unmolested
from the guts of decaying particles,
yet the same scientist thinks of neutrinos
as his wife shudders beneath his touch
and looks aside as his dog's dying eyes
sink into glacial pools of milk.

For the rest of us, when we think of this
fugitive time, we would like to nail
its heart to the floor and give it some pain.
We know that right now it runs by our houses,
smirking in the windows, and feel the fingers close
on the back of our necks, below the ears,
where the pumping of blood drones,
and see its moments as several fingers
squeezing in a heavyweight grip
with all the cards and a sadistic mind.
We call it the cheap pimp of death,
and locked in this wrestling match,
we can't find the imp behind the machine,
or see flowers growing in the sidewalk's cracks.

Yet, when two suns crisscross on their way
across the sky and the rocks signal quiet joy
to the gulls, the clam that shatters
by the drop from soaring air to sea ledge,
not only yields its smashed flesh
but offers a twinned darker glow of another passing
from the shell of the sky answered by stone.
The gull laughs knowingly at the welcome
of this other time of encounter, the time we can hear
when we pause on deserted beaches.

The second type of vibration held within
the dusky interior of relentless time,
only emerges in shattering,
when air and rock and sky and flesh seem to collide
but each is lost in the others,
shifting outside themselves, like when
the beam of the child's eye caught by cerulean,
laughing at the sky
hits yours
and you splinter in the reflected gleam,
and find yourself within caverns
you thought lost long ago.

Whenever we feel the throb of the neck
we imagine the grip and time's night,
and dream ourselves pursuing as superspies
saving our families from the international terrorist
whose explosives are concealed in all things.
Instead, the fears we send out collide with everything
since clumsy and unseeing, they lunge ahead,
convinced time will collect them, so they must hit first.
But, if we are lucky in how they smack their heads,
it is the fears that die, shattered
against the sight of the spring green of leaves
or the softness of skin pressed,
or by smells of the vaporous thicket of fruit stalls
at market. If we're really lucky, the gulls spot them
and drop them for us onto the rocks.

Only then do we come to the doggy knowledge
outside the realm of science that was in the eyes
when the tail wagged in recognition
of greeting the time of encounter. Its story
is found within the shade of all real meeting
and the blurring of hand on hand,
when the particles cease the straight lines
of decay and begin the round dance
about the glow of shimmering
and the soft and the pungent
and all things become a gesture
of fingers clasped and folded back
with others within themselves.

OTHER ANAPHORA LITERARY PRESS TITLES

Evidence and Judgment
By Lynn Clarke

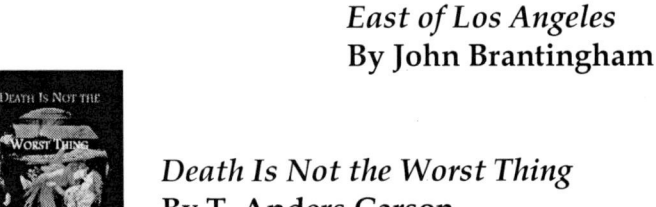

East of Los Angeles
By John Brantingham

Death Is Not the Worst Thing
By T. Anders Carson

The Seventh Messenger
By Carol Costa

Rain, Rain, Go Away...
By Mary Ann Hutchison

Truths of the Heart
By G. L. Rockey

Interviews with BFF Winners
By Anna Faktorovich, Ph.D.

Compartments
By Carol Smallwood

CPSIA information can be obtained at www.ICGtesting.com
Printed in the USA
BVOW022227280212

284048BV00001B/15/P

9 781937 536237